KATIE MORAG DELIVERS the MAIL

High Farm

The Holiday House

Mrs Bayview's

The Lady

The Redburn Bridge

The Village

THE ISLE of STRUAY

Grannie's

The Mainland

The Jetty

ISLE of STRUAY
SHOP & POST OFFICE

OBAN
TIMES
GET
YOUR COPY
HERE

The Shop & Post Office

A RED FOX BOOK : 978 0 099 26354 8

First published in Great Britain by The Bodley Head Children's Books 1984
Red Fox Mini Treasures edition published 1998

13 15 14 12

Copyright © Mairi Hedderwick 1984

Red Fox Books are published by Random House Children's Publishers UK
61-63 Uxbridge Road, London W5 5SA,
a division of The Random House Group Ltd.

Addresses for companies within The Random House Group Limited can
be found at: www.randomhouse.co.uk/offices.htm

THE RANDOM HOUSE GROUP Limited Reg No. 954009
www.randomhousechildrens.co.uk

A CIP catalogue record for this book is available from the British Library.

Printed in China

To all small places

KATIE MORAG
DELIVERS the MAIL

Mairi Hedderwick

Mini Treasures

RED FOX

Wednesdays were always hectic on the Isle of Struay, for that was the day that the boat brought mail and provisions from the mainland.

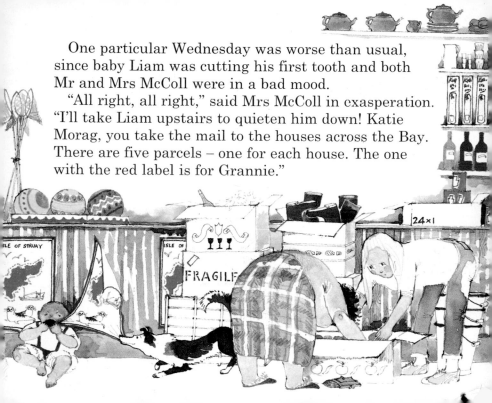

One particular Wednesday was worse than usual, since baby Liam was cutting his first tooth and both Mr and Mrs McColl were in a bad mood.

"All right, all right," said Mrs McColl in exasperation. "I'll take Liam upstairs to quieten him down! Katie Morag, you take the mail to the houses across the Bay. There are five parcels – one for each house. The one with the red label is for Grannie."

Pleased to escape, Katie Morag set off. She loved any excuse to visit her Grannie, who lived all alone in the very last house on the other side of the Bay.

But it was a hot day, and Katie Morag had just stopped for a moment to paddle in a pool beneath the Redburn Bridge, when suddenly – *splash!* – she slipped on a slithery stone and fell into the water, mailbag and all.

"Oh, dear! Oh, dear!" wailed Katie Morag, looking at the five soggy parcels. "All the addresses are smudged and I won't know which parcel is for which house now!"

Only Grannie's parcel was still recognizable by its red label.

Then, because she was so frightened and ashamed, Katie Morag did a silly thing. She ran the rest of the way to the other side of the Bay and threw a parcel – any parcel, except the red-labelled one – on to the doorstep of each of the first four houses. Nobody saw her. Still sobbing, she ran on to Grannie's.

"Well, this is a fine *boorach* you've got yourself into, Katie Morag," said Grannie, when Katie Morag had explained what she had done. "Still at least you've given me the right parcel – it's got the spare part for the tractor that I've been waiting for. I'll go and get the old grey lady going, while you dry yourself up. Then you can try and sort the whole muddle out."

Grannie had her head under the bonnet of the tractor for a long time. Occasionally, Katie Morag heard muffled words of anger and she thought of the angry words waiting for her at home...

Then, suddenly, with a cough of black smoke, the tractor stuttered into life and they set off to go round each of the four houses in turn.

The first house belonged to the Lady Artist.
She had been expecting tiny, thin brushes for her
miniature paintings, but the parcel Katie Morag had
left on her doorstep contained two enormous brushes.

"They're bigger than my painting boards!" she said
in disgust.

The second house was rented by the Holiday People.
They had ordered fishing hooks from a sports catalogue,
but their parcel had been full of garden seeds.

"We can't catch fish with daisies and lettuces!"
they complained.

At the third house, Mr MacMaster was standing by a big barrel of whitewash, holding the Lady Artist's paint brushes.

"How can I paint my walls with these fiddling little things?" he asked.

In the fourth house lived Mrs Bayview. "That stupid shop on the mainland! Where are my seeds? Flowers won't grow out of these," she said crossly, waving a packet of fishing hooks in the air.

After much trundling back and forth, Katie Morag finally managed to collect and deliver all the right things to all the right people.

Everyone smiled and waved and said, "Thank you very much."

By now it was getting dark. Katie Morag thought of the long journey home. She would be very late and her parents were so bad-tempered these days on account of Liam's noisy teething.

"Grannie, would you like to come back for tea?" she asked.

Katie Morag half hid behind Grannie as they walked in the kitchen door but, to her surprise, everyone was smiling. Liam had cut his tooth at last and all was calm.

"Thank you for helping out today, Katie Morag," said Mrs McColl. "Isn't she good, Grannie?"

"Och aye," said Grannie with a smile as she looked at Katie Morag. "She's very good at sorting things out, is our Katie Morag." And she said no more.